A Visit from St. Nicholas And Santa Mouse, Too!

Clement C. Mouse
Illustrated by Loretta Krupinski

SCHOLASTIC INC.

New York Toronto London Auckland Sydney
Mexico City New Delhi Hong Kong

'Twas the night before Christmas,
when all through the house
Not a creature was stirring,
except for a mouse;

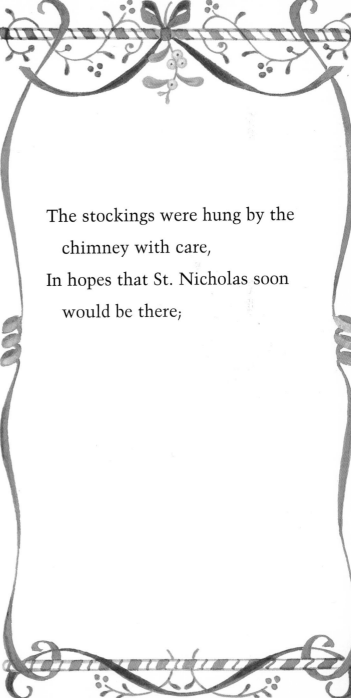

The stockings were hung by the
chimney with care,
In hopes that St. Nicholas soon
would be there;

The children were nestled all snug
 in their beds,
While visions of sugarplums
 danced in their heads;

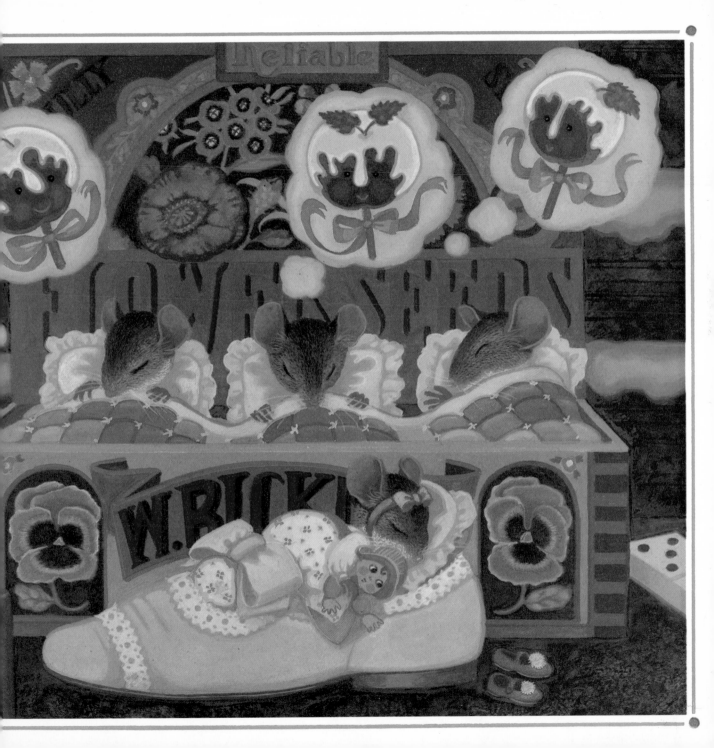

And Mamma in her kerchief,
and I in my cap,
Had just settled our brains
for a long winter's nap,

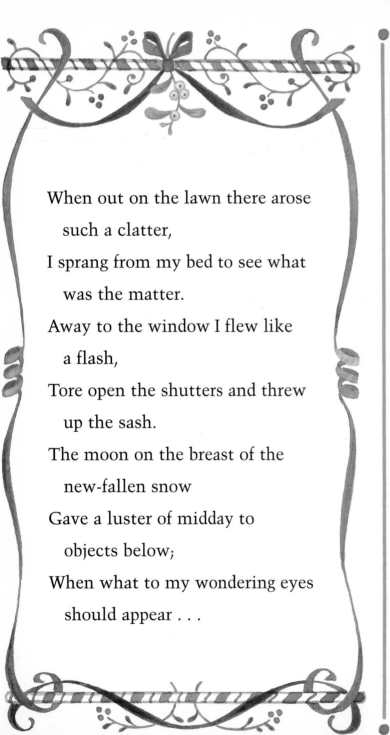

When out on the lawn there arose
   such a clatter,
I sprang from my bed to see what
   was the matter.
Away to the window I flew like
   a flash,
Tore open the shutters and threw
   up the sash.
The moon on the breast of the
   new-fallen snow
Gave a luster of midday to
   objects below;
When what to my wondering eyes
   should appear . . .

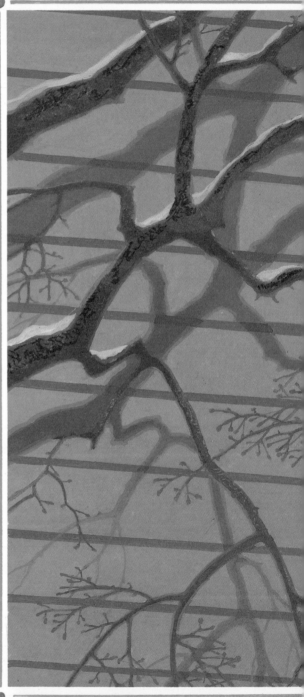

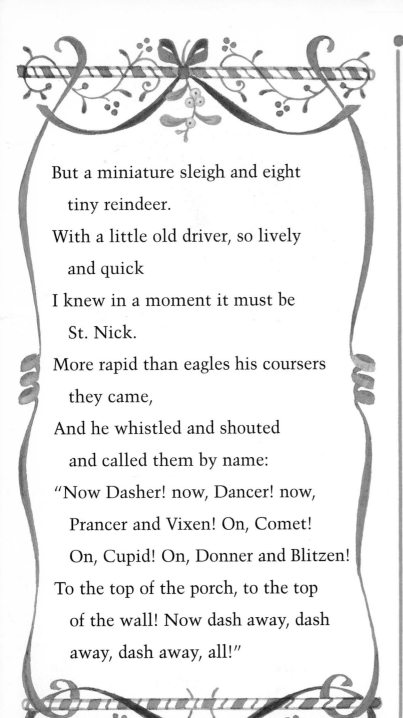

But a miniature sleigh and eight
   tiny reindeer.
With a little old driver, so lively
   and quick
I knew in a moment it must be
   St. Nick.
More rapid than eagles his coursers
   they came,
And he whistled and shouted
   and called them by name:
"Now Dasher! now, Dancer! now,
   Prancer and Vixen! On, Comet!
   On, Cupid! On, Donner and Blitzen!
To the top of the porch, to the top
   of the wall! Now dash away, dash
   away, dash away, all!"

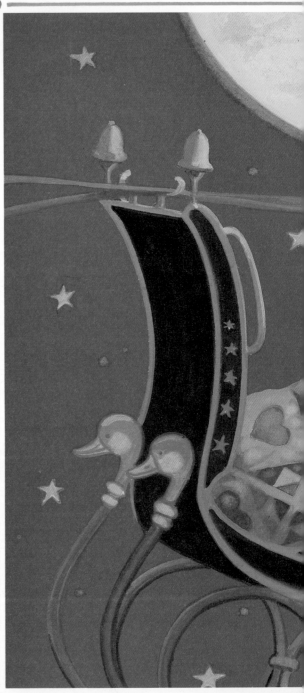

As dry leaves that before the wild
hurricane fly,
When they meet with an obstacle,
mount to the sky,
So up to the housetop the coursers
they flew,
With a sleigh full of toys,
and St. Nicholas, too.

And then in a twinkling I heard
on the roof
The prancing and pawing of each
little hoof.

As I drew in my head, and was
turning around,
Down the chimney St. Nicholas
came with a bound.

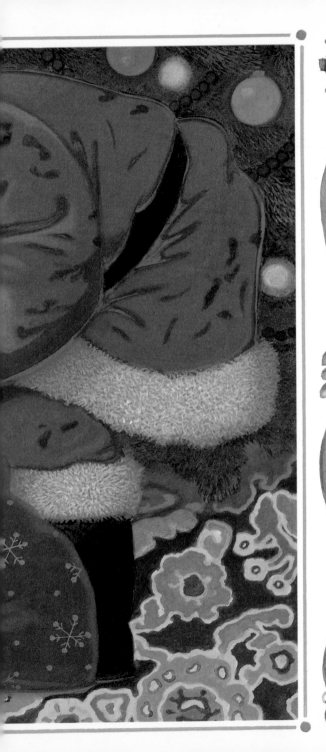

He was dressed all in fur from his head to his foot,
And his clothes were all tarnished with ashes and soot;
A bundle of toys he had flung on his back,
And he looked like a peddler just opening his pack.

His eyes, how they twinkled!
　His dimples, how merry!
His cheeks were like roses, his
　nose like a cherry;
His droll little mouth was drawn
　up like a bow,
And his whiskers and chin were
　as white as the snow.

The stump of a pipe he held tight
    in his teeth,
And the smoke, it encircled his
    head like a wreath.
He had a broad face and a little
    round belly
That shook when he laughed like
    a bowl full of jelly.

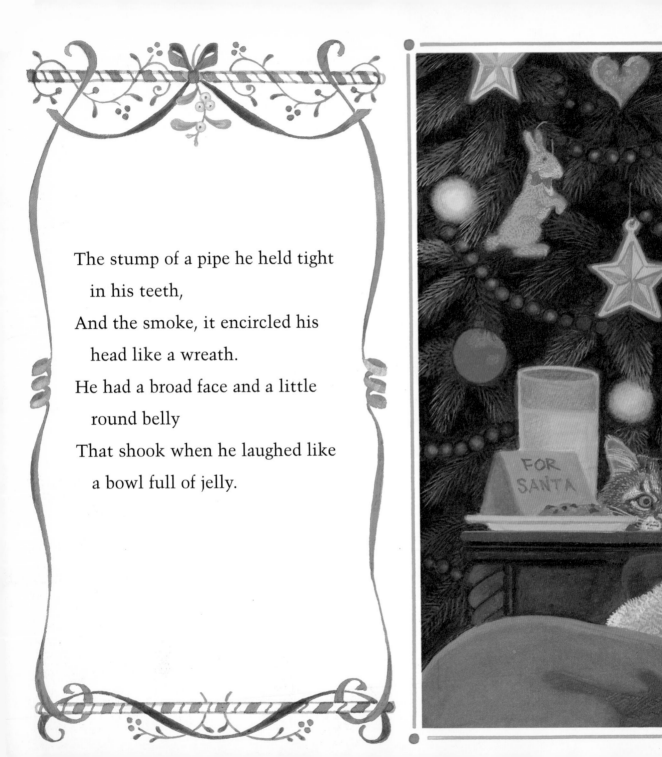

He was chubby and plump, a
right jolly old elf,
And I laughed when I saw him, in
spite of myself.
A wink of his eye and a twist of
his head
Soon gave me to know I had
nothing to dread.

He spoke not a word, but went straight to his work,
And filled all the stockings; then turned with a jerk,
And laying his finger aside of his nose,
And giving a nod, up the chimney he rose.

He sprang to his sleigh, to his
team gave a whistle,
And away they all flew like the
down of a thistle;
But I heard him exclaim, ere he
drove out of sight,

*"Happy Christmas
to all, and to all
A Good Night!"*

No part of this publication may be reproduced in whole or in part, or stored in a retrieval system, or transmitted in any form or by means, electronic, mechanical, photocopying, recording, or otherwise, without written permission of the publisher. For information regarding permission, write to Hyperion Books for Children, an imprint of Buena Vista Books, Inc., 114 Fifth Avenue, New York, NY 10011.

ISBN 0-439-13359-9

Illustrations copyright © 1998
by Loretta Krupinski.
All rights reserved.
Published by Scholastic Inc.,
555 Broadway, New York, NY 10012,
by arrangement with Hyperion Books for Children,
an imprint of Buena Vista Books, Inc..

12 11 10 9 8 7 6 5 4 3 2 1   9/9 0 1 2 3 4/0

Printed in the U.S.A.   24

First Scholastic printing, December 1999

The artwork for each picture was prepared using Gouache,
watercolor, and colored pencil.
The text for this book is set in 13-point Trump Medieval.